WEBCAM CHAT

AN EROTIC ADVENTURE

VICTORIA RUSH

VOLUME 13

JADE'S EROTIC ADVENTURES - BOOK 13

COPYRIGHT

FEEL THE RUSH:

Jade's Erotic Adventures – Book 1

When lonely divorcée Jade seeks to broaden her horizons, she's invited to a private dinner event which promises to stimulate all of her senses. Wearing nothing but masquerade masks, dinner guests receive special service under the table while their fellow diners look on...

The Dinner Party

Jade's Erotic Adventures - Book 2

Jade discovers an exotic adventure club where strangers meet to explore each other's bodies in mysterious dark rooms. Using special effects to project swirling light patterns onto their figures, the shifting shadows provide just enough illumination to highlight their naked bodies while protecting their identities...

The Dark Room

Jade's Erotic Adventures - Book 3

Jade discovers a yoga club where members stretch and explore each other's bodies in the buff. She books an appointment, and during the first session meets a young redhead who tantalizes her with her flexibility and stunning body...

Naked Yoga

For the uninhibited...

1
____

CYBERSURFING

After my playdate with the dominatrix, I felt I needed a breather to regain control over my sex life. My little excursion into the world of BDSM had been fun, but being whipped and hog-tied by a domme had its limits. Now it was *my* turn to set the terms of engagement. I wanted to be back in the driver's seat and branch out beyond one dominant partner.

One lonely night at home, I sat down in front of my computer and began searching for some online fun. I wanted something different from the run-of-the-mill porn—something more engaging. I needed something involving a live, two-way interaction. With a real person, someone with whom I could share a genuine, passionate, if only temporary, relationship. A virtual *fuck buddy*, for want of a better word.

I typed in the search words *webcam sex chat* and a bunch of listings popped up for live online chat. I clicked on one labeled *LiveGirls*, and a gallery of videos showing scantily-clad women touching themselves filled the screen. I tapped one of the thumbnails, where a live stream showed a pretty girl lying facedown on a bed, wearing only a thong. As she swayed her hips from side to side, she looked over her shoulder suggestively toward the camera. Beside the video window, a flurry of comments filled the chat box.

Spread your legs, someone named bigjohn said.

Nice ass, hornyjoe commented.

Can I see your tits? guest34 pleaded.

All the while, the pretty brunette ran her hands across her concealed breasts and rolled her hips in the same robotic manner. For a moment, I was hypnotized like everyone else by her lithe and sexy body. But as attractive as she was, I had no interest in joining what amounted to a public strip show. I was just about to exit the screen when I noticed a button for Private Chat.

Let's see if she's any more engaging one-on-one, I thought.

I clicked the button and a Join Now window covered the stream.

Jeesuz, I cursed. They never make this easy.

I filled in the required fields for Username, Password, and E-mail, then clicked the button. The next screen presented me with a choice between selecting ten free credits or buying a package of credits starting at fifty dollars.

So that's how it works, I thought. *It's not much different from a real strip club. As long as you're stuffing their stockings with cash, the girls are happy to put on a show for you.*

I'd never paid for sex of any kind, and I wasn't about to get started now. I didn't want to chat with someone who was only in it for the money. I backtracked to the main search screen and adjusted my search phrase to *free amateur sex chat* and clicked Enter.

A fresh set of listings popped up, including an intriguing one named *SexRoulette — free webcam live chat*. When I clicked on the link, a window came up with two side-by-side blank video screens. I enabled my laptop cam and mic, then I clicked the Start button. Suddenly, a live feed of me sitting half-naked in my bathrobe appeared in the left window, while some naked guy stroking his dick appeared in the right window.

Horrified to see that my face was showing, I quickly tilted my screen down and cursed out loud.

What's the matter? the naked guy typed in the chat box. *You're very pretty. Can I see your face again?*

I paused for a moment, realizing that he could hear me, then I clicked the microphone button to mute my mic. I wasn't prepared to carry on a live audio conversation with some naked guy. For that matter, I wasn't interested in carrying on a sex chat with *any* man.

I clicked the Next button and a different naked guy appeared with his legs spread wide apart, revealing another erect, throbbing cock. Every time I clicked Next, a different naked man appeared, pulling on his pud. As amusing as I found the experience of scrolling through a bunch of men's penises, the thought of chatting with one of these nameless guys turned my stomach.

Where were all the girls? I thought. *Are only guys interested in naughty online chats?*

I scanned the site and noticed some links across the top for different chat rooms. The default setting was for Mixed, but I could also choose between Guys, Girls, and Couples. Intrigued, I clicked on the Couples link, and a new window popped up showing a woman bobbing her head between a man's knees while his hand typed on a computer keyboard beside him on the bed.

Hi, the man typed in the chat window. *Wanna play?*

I paused for a moment, wondering if it might be fun to watch a hetero couple going at it.

Maybe some other time, I typed, before clicking on the Girls tab.

A new window popped up requiring me to verify that I was over eighteen years of age (*only to view girls??*) then I was redirected to a different website showing the familiar gallery of naked girls from the LiveGirls site. When I clicked on one of the images, a similar video and chat screen appeared. Another pretty young girl perched half-naked on a bed, while a bunch of anonymous viewers made lewd comments, 'tipping' her occasionally with tokens. Whenever anybody tipped her enough tokens, she bent over and waved her ass in front of the camera.

What the fuck? I thought. *Is it only professional girls who want to chat online?*

I clicked out of the website and was about to pull my vibrator out of my nightstand for some quiet alone time, when I decided to give it one last try.

There's got to be other lonely girls who are looking for a quick hookup with like-minded women.

I went back to the main search page and typed in *lesbian online chat.* Near the top of the listings, I noticed a site titled *SapphicChat — girls only free online chat.*

That's what I'm talking about, I said out loud, clicking the link.

Another side-by-side video setup appeared on the screen with a chat box underneath. I enabled my cam and carefully positioned my laptop lid so that only my torso was visible, then I pulled my robe tightly around my neck to cover myself up. There'd be no more skin showing until I was able to qualify a suitable candidate.

I clicked the Start button, and within a few seconds the adjacent window flickered with a live stream showing a fat woman lying on her bed with her droopy boobs hanging down by her waist.

Yikes, I said, quickly clicking the Next button. I felt bad judging the visitors so harshly, but it wasn't much different from other dating apps. If you didn't feel the chemistry right away, everybody just moved on.

After a few seconds, a new image filled the sender window. This time an older woman sat in front of her computer with her elbows propped up on her desk. Deep folds of flesh hung from her neck and upper chest as she peered sadly into the screen.

Wow, I thought. *These online forums really bring out the lonely girls.*

I toggled through the list of online visitors until an image appeared showing a younger girl sitting cross-legged on her bed, wearing a tight V-neck sweater. Her breasts were full and plump, and although her face was partially hidden off-screen, I could tell from the downiness of her bare legs in a mid-thigh skirt that she was considerably younger than me. I parted my legs unconsciously as my pussy throbbed in excitement.

Finally. A sexy girl who wants an authentic online chat.

ASL? I typed, wanting to be sure she was of legal age. The last thing I needed was to have the police breaking down my door for engaging a minor in online sex.

19, curious, Houston, she typed. *You?*

Nineteen? She barely looked of age. I'd have to vet her more carefully if things went much further.

I paused for a moment, wondering how I wanted to present myself. I didn't want to scare her away by revealing my true age if she was looking to hook up with someone younger. But she had to lean at least a little bit toward girls if she'd engaged me this far.

28, bi, Milwaukee, I stretched the facts on all three aspects.

She paused for a moment holding her hand over her computer keyboard, then the video screen suddenly went blank and a new visitor came online.

Touché, I thought. *I guess this works both ways. My fellow online surfers can be just as rash and judgmental as me when it comes to who they find attractive.*

Obviously. I hadn't measured up in her eyes. But had I been too old, not the right sexual orientation, or was it my *body* she didn't like?

I peered at my image in my webcam feed and looked at my tightly-bound boobs wrapped up in my bathrobe. I'd been slouching a bit, and the heavy terrycloth robe wasn't doing much justice to the shape of my bosom. I spread the lapels of my robe a few inches apart and lifted my chest. My ample cleavage shone through the opening, revealing the roundness of my breasts.

That looks better, I smiled, nodding at the sexy reflection. *If this doesn't hook them, I'm really losing my mojo.*

The next visitor appeared to be another young girl seated on a chair in front of her computer. She only showed the lower half of her face, but from her tight skin and smooth neck muscles, she looked to be in her late teens or early twenties. Her tight T-shirt had a wishbone-shaped "C" emblem on the front. In the background, two small double beds sat on either side of her small room.

Hi, I typed, deciding to take a more measured approach with this new visitor. *What brings you to this crazy place so late at night?*

Just bored I guess, she responded.

Me too, I said. *This is my first time doing something like this. I'm used to meeting people the old-fashioned way.*

Boys or girls? she typed.

It was obvious that she was fishing. I had no idea what the right answer was, so I decided to play it safe.

Both, I guess. But I prefer girls. How about you?

I like boys... she typed. *But lately I've been finding myself unusually attracted to my dorm mate.*

Oh, I said, happy to hear she tilted both ways. *Where do you go to school?*

University of Chicago.

My heart skipped a beat when I realized how close she was to me in the real world.

What are you studying? I said, trying to steady my nervous hand as I typed.

I'm enrolled in the BA program, so right now it's mostly liberal arts. I'm just in my first year, so I haven't really decided on my major yet. I'm thinking maybe Communications...

She's barely eighteen! I thought. *My pussy throbbed at the thought of uncovering more of this pretty co-ed.*

What kind of career were you thinking of?

I dunno. Public relations, marketing, maybe television.

On the production side?

I suppose so. Somewhere behind the camera. I don't think I have prime time face.

You should let other people be the judge of that. From what I can see so far, I think you're very pretty. The combination of good looks and good communication skills will give you quite a leg up in that field.

Thanks, she said, tilting the camera up a little higher on her face. She smiled a broad smile, revealing perfectly-straight, pearly-white teeth. *What about you, what do you do?*

I'm a freelance graphic designer.

So you design websites and stuff like that?

A little bit of that. But I do more corporate work like logos, editorial layouts, that sort of thing.

That sounds interesting, the girl said. *I guess we both have an interest in communications of sorts...*

I paused for a moment, wondering how much longer I wanted to focus on the professional sides of our lives.

It looks like we share an interest in another form of communicating too. ;-)

LOL. This isn't the kind of communications my profs talk about.

I'm a little surprised to hear that, I said. *The world is rapidly adopting new forms of social media every day. Perhaps you can consider this as a type of vocational training.*

Except most people who come to this website are interested in only one thing.

You mean meeting people? I teased.

In a manner of speaking...

Are you testing the waters here because of your roommate?

Maybe. I didn't realize I had such a strong attraction to girls until I met her.

Have you shared your feelings with her?

Gawd no. She has a boyfriend. It could get very uncomfortable around here if I came on to her too strongly. We have to share this small room for the rest of the year and perhaps for the rest of our college residency.

Two charged up bodies in a small space can make for a combustible mixture. Do you think she's attracted to you also?

Not by the way I've seen her and her boyfriend go at it. I can't tell you how many times I've come back to my room to find a sock on the door.

Poor thing, I thought. *It doesn't sound like she's got much of an outlet to express her real feelings. I better tread lightly.*

Maybe you just need to be a little more suggestive when you have some alone time with her. You know, wear skimpier clothes to bed, come back from the shower naked. That sort of thing. If she's interested, she'll soon let you know.

It sounds like you have a little more experience with girls, she said. *Are you lesbian?*

Now we're getting to the crux of it, I thought. It was kind of fun playing the role of the girl's online mentor.

They say everyone's somewhere on the continuum, I said. *I'd say I'm about a nine, but I seem to be moving more to the right with each passing year. Men don't really do it for me any longer.*

The chat window paused for a moment as the girl seemed to process what I said.

What's it like? she said. *You know, being with a woman?*

Crikey, I thought. *How do I answer that without sounding like some kind of stalker?*

That's an interesting question. It's different in so many ways. Woman like different things than men. We're more focused on building the relationship. Men are mostly just interested in sex.

Aren't women interested in that too?

Yes, of course, I laughed. *We just let it happen more —organically.*

Organically?

We let it happen naturally, as our feelings for one another grow stronger. Instead of just jumping on the biscuit, in a manner of speaking.

You mean kind of like what we're doing right now?

I was beginning to feel a strange attraction to this girl. Beyond the pretty outside package, she had a sweet innocence to her.

I suppose, I said. *We lesbians generally like to get to know our partner a little better before jumping into bed with them.*

Do you mind my asking how that works when you do get together? I mean, it's not like regular boy-girl coupling...

All this tip-toeing around the edges of sexy talk was

beginning to stir some new feelings inside me. I was enjoying the process of educating this young girl on the nuances of lesbian relationships.

It's not so different, when it comes right down to it. We have the same sensitive parts. We just use them a little differently.

Do you miss the penetration aspect of the relationship?

Maybe it's time to stop being so nuanced, I thought.

Who says we have to forego the penetration aspect?

Oh, sorry—the girl said, as I saw a flush roll over her face. *It's just that without a penis involved in the equation...*

There are lots of ways us girls can enjoy penetration without a man. Strap-on dildos, two-sided phalluses, using sex toys. I'm guessing you've tried one or two of these before?

Well, yes. I have a vibrator I play with when my roommate is away. But I had no idea women used them together like you said.

Oh, yes. There are lots of interesting ways we make our own fun.

You're getting me pretty worked up talking about it. Can you tell me how you use a two-sided phallus?

Suddenly I became acutely aware of the wetness that had been accumulating between my legs. This innocent but sexy banter had been getting *both* of us worked up.

Well, usually it starts with us lying on our backs with our butts facing one another...

Mmm, the girl typed.

Fuck! I thought. *It's happening. I'm actually seducing a young college girl online!*

Then we insert the two ends in each of our pussies and push our bodies together...

The girl's left hand wandered below my line of vision as she began to squirm in her seat while pecking her keyboard with her other hand.

All the way? she asked. *Do you touch your bodies together?*

Usually, if the dildo isn't too long. That's where it really gets fun. There's nothing so electrifying as feeling your lover's peachka pressed up against your own.

God, that's so hot!

And wet. ;-)

You're making me very wet right now.

I spread my legs and began strumming my clit with my fingers at the thought of the pretty co-ed getting turned on by my explanation.

Are you touching yourself? I said.

Yes. Are you?

I am now.

I wish I could touch you the way you're describing right now.

If I could reach out through my screen, believe me, I would. I'd love to show you what it feels like to make love to a woman.

Can I see your breasts? They look very full and sexy.

I thought you'd never ask.

I pulled my robe apart and let the shawl fall around my shoulders.

OMG! the girl typed. *They're gorgeous. Do you mind if I ask how old you are? Because those are the most beautiful tits I think I've ever seen.*

I paused for a moment trying to decide how young I wanted to pretend to be. The last thing I wanted to do in the heat of the action was scare away another online partner because she thought I was too old.

Everybody tells me I look ten years younger than my real age, I thought. *She'll never know.*

That's very kind of you, I said. *I'm twenty-five. But before we go any further, I should probably ask you the same. If you're in your first year of college, you must be barely legal.*

I turned eighteen two months ago.

Like I said. Barely legal.

We're two consenting adults.

Since we're getting to know each other so intimately, can I ask your name? I don't want to have sex with a faceless, nameless person.

I'm Holly.

Pleased to meet you Holly. My name's Jade.

That's a lovely name.

Yours too, I said. *Holly and Jade. I like the way they go together.*

I'm imagining us going together in more ways than one.

Damn, girl, you're making me soaking wet. Can I see a bit more of you too? I want to let my mind run all over your sweet body.

The girl reached up over her shoulders and pulled her T-shirt over her head. Then she reached behind her back and unclasped her bra. When she pulled it off her shoulders and threw it on the floor, I gasped. Her breasts were smaller than mine, but stood firm and erect on her chest. But far more fascinating, was their *shape.* They were far pointier than most, pressing straight out toward me like two fleshy obelisks.

Mmm, I typed. *Those are mighty succulent boobies you have, Holly.*

Not as full and appetizing as yours! she returned.

I love their shape. I could suck on your pointy nipples all day!

I'd like that, Holly said. *You're going to make me cum pretty soon if you keep talking to me like that.*

That's not the only part of you that I want to suck, I said, starting to rub my clit more quickly. *I want to take your sweet nub into my mouth and watch your twist all over my face.*

Yes, Jade. I want you to suck my clit. Make me cum all over your face.

Oh Baby, I said. *Let me see and feel you cum. I'm pressing *my fingers inside you now...*

Fuck, Jade. I can feel you inside me. I'm going to cum...

As I watched Holly writhing in her chair, my mouth opened unconsciously, imagining her riding my face.

Yes, baby, I said. *Cum in my mouth. Let it go.*

Suddenly, a deep flush spread over Holly's chest and she began jerking wildly in her chair.

Ohhhhhhh, she typed. *I'm cumming Jade!*

I hadn't been concentrating very much on my own feelings up to this point, but when I saw Holly coming, I thrust my fingers deep into my pussy and gushed all over my hand. While I watched her jerking in her chair, my tits jiggled spastically on my chest as the tremors spread throughout my body.

After a long pause, Holly began to type again.

That was incredible! she said. *I haven't had an orgasm that powerful in a long time.*

You should try this girl thing more often, I typed. *It's even better in real life. Maybe you and your roommate can find a way—*

Suddenly, Holly's face turned to the side and a panicked expression fell over her face.

I think she's here! she typed. *Someone's at the door!*

Oh no—not now, I thought. *Just when we were establishing such a strong connection.* I banged away at my keyboard, fearful of losing her forever.

Can we do this again some—

Holly's video stream suddenly went dark as she signed out of the program. I was sad to see her go, but at the same time I was thrilled to have made such an exhilarating connection my first time online.

I'm going to have to try this again very soon, I thought, closing my laptop with sticky fingers.

2

FULL DISCLOSURE

After my chat with Holly ended so abruptly, I stayed online for more than an hour hoping she'd reconnect and continue our conversation. But I knew that if her roommate had returned to their dorm, she'd be hard-pressed to find any privacy for the rest of the night. Their single room was so tiny that it would be impossible to find any place for a private conversation, let alone an online sex chat.

For the rest of the night, I fantasized about her roommate barging in to find her masturbating in front of her computer, then tearing off her clothes to join the innocent college girl in her lesbian discovery. If anything could persuade a straight girl to stray to the other side, surely it would be the sight of the winsome co-ed getting off watching other naked women. I came many times that night imagining all the fun the two of them might have discovering the joys of lesbian lovemaking for the first time.

The following night, I was eager to get back online to see if I could reconnect with Holly. Even though I knew my chances were slim, if she found herself alone again and was in a similar frame of mind, I hoped she might have the same idea. Around the same time that evening, I logged back into the SapphicChat site and began toggling through the gallery of online visitors.

I found a few interesting candidates, and for a short time I engaged in some playful banter with a closeted housewife from Texas, then a curious divorcée from California, then a sexy dyke from Delaware. On any other day, I might have been enticed to remove my clothing and begin another erotic online encounter, but after a few minutes of superficial conversation, I found myself clicking the Next button in search of my innocent college girl.

I was just about to reengage with the Texas housewife when a familiar silhouette filled the visitor chat window. She was sitting cross-legged in the middle of her bed wearing a tight T-shirt and shorts with her face out of the frame, but I recognized the contour of her breasts instantly. Her pointy tits pressed against the soft fabric of her shirt, barely concealing the two tubers of mouthwatering flesh. My pussy throbbed at the sight of the familiar swellings.

Holly? I typed on my keyboard.

Who's this? she responded in the chat box. I was wearing a different outfit this evening, and with my face off-camera, it was obvious she didn't recognize me.

It's Jade. I've been thinking about you so much since our chat last night.

She stretched her legs out on opposite sides of her laptop and leaned her body forward to type on her keyboard. This only accentuated the elongated shape of her breasts, highlighting the meaty areolas at their tips.

Me too. I wasn't sure if I'd find you again. Sorry for cutting you off so suddenly last night.

I completely understand. Did your roommate catch you in the act?

I was able to get myself pulled together pretty quickly. But she must have sensed something was up from the look on my face. Plus, I'm sure the room was saturated with the scent of my sex by the time we finished.

The thought of Holly's scent filling the room made my pussy weep, and I spread my legs unconsciously, feeling the moisture between my legs.

Did you tell her what you'd been doing?

No, I made up some lame-ass excuse about researching a term paper.

Too bad. If anything might swing her the other way, it would be the sight of her pretty roommate getting off watching other girls.

I dunno. I'm still afraid what she might think. I could smell her boyfriend's cologne all over her when she came back. I don't think she's interested in me that way.

Give it time. It's still early in the semester. She probably just needs to get a bit more comfortable around you. Your irresistible personality will eventually win her over.

So you're saying my body's not enough? ;-)

Don't be silly. Your figure is exquisite. I paused for a moment, contemplating whether to take our online conversation to the next level. *Though I still haven't seen your entire face. Don't you think we've come far enough to show the rest of our bodies to one another?*

Holly hesitated with her hands over her keyboard. For a moment, I thought she might hit the Exit button in fear of revealing her real identity.

I guess so, she said. *But I'm kind of wary about my showing my face in a public forum like this. You never know who might be recording us. I'd be horrified if somebody posted this online and my parents saw a clip of me masturbating online one day.*

I know how you feel, I typed. *I've been having the same concerns. Why don't we open a separate private chat. Do you have Skype?*

Yes, Holly said. *I use it to chat with my folks every couple of weeks.*

What's your username? Mine's gigi84.

Is that the year you were born? I thought you said you were twenty-five!

Ok, full disclosure, I sheepishly typed. *I might have stretched my age a little bit. But everyone tells me I look much younger than I really am.*

It's cool, Holly said. *Everybody has a secret identity online. I never would have guessed your age. You certainly have the body of a 25 yr old!*

Sexy enough to entice a college girl into an online affair with a middle-aged woman?

That's not middle-aged! You're barely through the first trimester. But to answer your question, yes. My Skype ID is ucgrad22.

LOL. I'm trying to slow down the clock and you're already looking ahead. Shall we log out of here and start a new Skype chat?

C u in a few minutes, sexy momma! Holly said, signing off with a playful kissing emoji.

As her image disappeared from the video window, my pussy pitter-pattered at her playful description of me. I couldn't wait to have her all to myself on a private webcam link, and I quickly exited the webpage and signed into Skype. I searched for *ucgrad22* and a profile pulled up with a thumbnail image of a pretty teenager wearing sunglasses against a seaside background. I clicked on the image and a new chat window opened, giving me three options. I could leave a text message in the chat box at the bottom of the screen, or I could send her an audio or video call request.

What the hell, I thought. *I think we're well past the preliminaries.*

I tapped on the video button and as my video stream went live, the sound of an electronic call warbled through my speakers. While I waited for Holly to pick up on the other end, I adjusted the angle of my camera so that it focused with a close-up of my face. I'd chosen to wear some skimpy lingerie this evening, and I didn't want to be too presumptuous right out of the gate. Besides, I was eager to see Holly's full face, and I figured if I set the tone, that she might follow.

After a few seconds, the bottom half of the screen filled with the familiar image of Holly's chest in her tight T-shirt. I smiled when I saw her, and she quickly tilted her screen up so that I could see her face also. My heart immediately began accelerating, not only because she appeared so close, but also because she was absolutely stunning. She had large doe-eyes, a cute upturned nose, and long auburn hair falling over her shoulders. With her bright green eyes and sprinkling of little freckles, she looked like a dead-ringer for the actress Emma Stone.

"Can you hear me?" I spoke toward my laptop's onboard microphone.

"Yes," Holly replied. "Oh my God, Jade—you're gorgeous!"

"Not bad for a thirty-five-year-old?" I smiled.

"Not bad for a twenty-five-year-old!" Holly beamed back at me.

"You're not too shabby yourself, young lady," I said.

"Those eyes are to die for. Has anyone ever told you that you look a bit like—"

"Yes, I know. Emma Stone. I get it all the time. I think it's just the red hair and freckles. We gingers are always getting compared to one another. Amy Adams, Bryce Howard, Lindsay Lohan—I've heard them all."

"Sorry," I said. "I didn't mean to compare you to anybody. You're gorgeous and unique in your own right."

"No worries. It's just that I used to get teased quite a lot when I was younger."

"Not so much anymore, I bet."

"Thankfully, I seem to be outgrowing it."

"I bet you turn a lot of heads from both boys and girls on campus."

"I haven't been paying much attention. I've been focusing primarily on my studies. I don't get out much..."

"Oh my God, girl. You don't know what you're missing. With a face and body like that, you could have your pick of the litter. You could make your roommate super-jealous by bringing home a hot new boyfriend every night of the week."

"Except I'm not really into guys right now. Though I will confess, I *was* fantasizing about phalluses most of the night."

"Oh? Do tell. Real or pretend ones?"

"All your talk about strap-on dildos and double-sided cocks got me worked up all night. As soon as Jen left in the morning, I took out my vibrator and have been playing with it most of the day."

My pussy throbbed at the thought of Holly jilling herself with a dildo, as I felt a dribble of lubrication run down the crack of my ass.

"Same here. Do you have a favorite?"

Holly leaned over her bed and reached into the night

table beside her bed. She pulled out a plain flesh-colored plastic dildo and held it in front of the screen for me to see.

"I just have this one. I actually pulled it out of the trash can at my house a few years ago. I think it belonged to my mother. I've been too nervous to go to an adult store to look for one of my own."

"Jeesuz, girl," I said, staring at the prehistoric sex toy. "That looks like something straight out of the eighties. Vibrators have become a lot more sophisticated over the last few years."

I reached into my side table and pulled out my favorite rabbit vibrator and held it up for Holly to see.

"This is one of my favorites. It's called The Rabbit. It twists and rolls on the end to provide an exquisite form of internal stimulation. But best of all are these little rabbit ears."

I tweaked the two silicone flaps with my fingers.

"When you turn it on, they vibrate and flap directly against your clitoris, providing the most intense type of stimulation you can imagine. The whole thing is made of super-soft silicone, so it almost feels like the real thing when it's inside you."

Holly stared at the multi-colored vibrator with wide eyes, then glanced back at her plain plastic dildo.

"I'm feeling pretty inadequate right now. Can you show me how it works? I mean—just turn it on so I can see how it moves?"

"Of course," I said, happy to indulge Holly's curiosity.

I held the vibrator vertical and turned it sideways so she could see the rabbit ears in profile view, then turned the device on. As it began making a low humming sound, a circle of beads swirled just under the transparent surface.

"See these circulating beads? They provide a sensation unlike any man can deliver."

Emma stared at the strange contraption and nodded.

"I can imagine. How else does it move?"

I pressed another button, and the tip of the dildo started rolling in small circles.

"Holy shit!" Holly exclaimed, with wide eyes. "That thing really is unlike any other cock, isn't it?"

"So you *have* experienced a real penis, then?" I said, probing for more details about her sex life.

"Well yes, just a few times in high school with a boyfriend in my senior year. But he wasn't endowed nearly as well as that thing!"

"It's a little bigger than most men's cocks, I suppose. But here's the best part." I tapped another button on the base of the vibrator and the rabbit ears started fluttering against the side of the shaft. "Can you see that," I said, pointing toward the flickering ears. "That's something else no man's cock can hope to emulate. The combined effect of these three actions will send you over the moon."

"Oh my God," Holly said. "I'm already soaking wet at the thought of having that thing inside me. I don't suppose you'd be willing to demonstrate it working for real? I mean —*inside* you?"

By this time, the insides of my thighs were coated with slippery lubrication emanating from my pussy and my clit was burning in need of some direct stimulation.

"It would be my pleasure—literally."

I unplugged my laptop and carried it with my vibrator to my bed. Then I sat up with my back resting against the headboard and placed the laptop between my legs about two feet away so Holly could see my entire body from my hips to my head.

"Mmm, I like what you're wearing tonight," Holly said, admiring my lacy camisole and matching boy-shorts panties.

"I wore it just for you," I purred, cupping my breasts and pinching my nipples through the thin fabric.

"I wish I were there to touch you like that. I want to caress every square inch of your body."

"Likewise," I said, spreading my legs further apart. "Can you take your T-shirt off so I can see your beautiful breasts while I play with myself? I've been fantasizing about seeing you naked again for the last twenty-four hours."

"Absolutely," Holly said. "In fact, let me get completely naked so I can enjoy myself properly while I'm watching you."

Holly pulled her shirt over her head as her pointy tits jiggled on her chest. Then she raised her ass and pulled her shorts over her ankles, revealing a completely bare pussy.

"Oh my God, Holly," I gasped, staring at her sexy slit and puffy labia. "Just when I thought you couldn't get any more perfect. That might be the prettiest pussy I've ever seen."

"I bet you say that to all the girls," she teased.

"I have to admit that I love every woman's vulva. But yours looks unusually—*pristine*. Almost like it's never been touched. Are you sure you've been with boys before?"

"Only a few times," Holly laughed. "Not as many times as I've used my vibrator."

"Well that skinny little thing isn't much thicker than a toothbrush. No wonder you look like you've barely been touched down there."

"My boyfriend in high school was pretty small too. I didn't know they came any bigger. Show me how that big dildo fills you up, Jade."

I had planned on giving Holly a slow striptease to get

her in the mood, but when started talking dirty, I practically tore my panties and camisole off.

Holly paused for a moment as her eyes darted over her screen, appraising my body.

"Holy fuck, Jade! *You're* the one with the perfect body. I'd die to have your curves. You look like something straight out of some men's magazine centerfold."

"Or *women's*," I chuckled. "Hopefully this body works for both sides of the aisle."

Holly traced her right hand down the front of her stomach and began circling her fingers over her clit.

"It's definitely working *this* side of the aisle, I can assure you."

"Mmm, Holly, you're making me very wet."

"Wet enough for that big dildo to slide up inside you?"

"Let's see," I said, placing the end of the vibrator against my opening. I tapped the oscillating function button and the tip of the dildo began rolling over my slippery labia. As I began to insert the dildo inside my hole, Holly leaned in closer to the screen.

"Damn," she panted. "My boyfriend's cock never did anything like that. It was mostly straight in-and-out action. Usually pretty fast."

"You have no idea how good real lovemaking can be," I purred. "The trick is to take your time and let the passion slowly build. Only after you've been properly teased and stimulated, is it time for a pounding. The pleasure is so much more intense when you let it build to a boil."

"You're sure bringing me to a boil right now," Holly said, rolling her fingers over her slit. "Show me how you enjoy the rest of that special dildo. I want to watch you squirm and moan."

I raised my knees higher off the bed and tapped the

second button on the vibrator. As the rotating silver beads glistened in the nightlight from my side table, the shaft slowly disappeared inside my cavern as I pushed it further inside me.

"Fuck that's hot!" Holly panted, her big doe eyes widening even further. "What does that feel like inside you?"

"It's like nothing else," I moaned. "The feeling of the beads caressing the inside of my walls while the rotating tip presses against my G-spot is simply indescribable. You've got to get one of these for yourself to truly appreciate it."

"I'll be going to my corner sex shop as soon as it opens tomorrow," Holly grunted, slipping her fingers inside her pussy. "You've certainly sold me."

"Just don't get too attached to it," I said. "It's still doesn't compare to the delicate touch of a real live, sensuous woman."

"But you said I can *combine* both sensations, with the right kind of vibrator. I might buy me one of those two-sided dildos while I'm at the store, just in case the opportunity ever arises with my roommate..."

With that image dancing around my head, I shoved the vibrator deep inside me and tapped on the rabbit ears button. As the ears began flapping against my burning clit, I humped my hips forward and back, pressing the dildo in and out of me.

"That's a sight I'd love to see," I panted, feeling the vibrations emanating throughout my body.

"I'll see if it can be arranged," Holly said, suddenly picking up her plastic vibrator and thrusting it inside her. "That is, if I can ever get past first base with her. I bet she'd enjoy watching you as much as I do. Maybe we can arrange our own little ménage à trois."

"Without her boyfriend, you mean?"

"*Definitely* without him," Holly moaned. "No boys allowed."

Holly and I watched each other holding our dildos with two hands as we fucked ourselves with increasing urgency.

"I'd like that," I panted. "But not nearly as much as being there for real. I want to feel your body pressed up against mine and make you scream in pleasure."

"You're getting pretty close to making me do that right now," Holly moaned, rolling her hips while she stared at her screen. "I'm getting close. Do you think you can cum with me?"

"Fuck yes," I grunted. "Any time. Just tell me when."

"First tell me what you want to do with me. When we get together."

"Oh Holly," I moaned, daring myself to think the unthinkable. "Everything. I want to kiss you and suck you and fuck you with every ounce of my being. We'll take our time and make it last. I'd make love to you all day long if I could."

"How do you want to fuck me, Jade?" Holly panted as her body began tensing up. The pupils in her eyes had become large and dark, signaling that she was nearing her peak. "Will you fuck me with your strap-on dildo or two-headed prick?"

"Yes," I moaned, getting even more turned on by her dirty talk. "I'll fuck you until you come all over my big dildo. I'll make you gush all over my cock while I fuck you in every imaginable way—"

"Yes, Jade," Holly groaned. "I want to feel you inside me. Make me cum all over your big dildo."

Holly was humping her hips wildly now against her plastic dildo, pumping it in and out of her pussy as her breathing became more jagged. I pressed the vibrating rabbit ears hard up against my clit and thrust my vibrator as deep inside me as I could. Within seconds, I could feel the insides of my pussy beginning to expand in preparation for a hard orgasm.

"Cum for me, baby," I groaned, feeling the first waves of passion roll over me. "Press your pussy against me and cum with me. I feel you Holly—"

"Jade!" Holly suddenly screamed, as her hips started shaking in spastic spasms. "I'm cumming!"

Her whole body began convulsing as her pointy breasts shook in tiny tremors.

"Oh baby," I growled, extending my tongue trying to reach her jiggling tits. "Mummy's coming with you. Feel me filling you up. Cum all over my big cock. Let me feel your tight pussy clamping down on me."

"Fuck yes," Holly hissed, holding her spear tightly inside her while her hips convulsed on the bed in front of her computer screen. "I'm still cumming. Oh Jade—"

Suddenly I heard the sound of a door swinging open and another girl's voice.

"What the fuck?" the girl's voice said. "I'm so sorry, Holly. I'll come back later—"

"No," Holly pleaded, peering up from the screen. "Don't leave, Jen. I've been thinking of you..."

Holly glanced down at her screen and gave me a sweet smile, then her video suddenly went blank.

Maybe she'll be getting her wish sooner than she hoped, I thought, pulling the still-throbbing vibrator out of my pussy.

THREE'S A CROWD

For the longest time, I stared at the empty screen, imagining what was happening in Holly's dorm room. Her roommate had surprised her in the throes of orgasm, with her naked body splayed in front of her computer and a vibrator deeply embedded in her pussy. How could anyone respond to such a sight?

There were only three possible scenarios. Either her roommate had turned tail and quickly exited the room, closing the door behind her. Or she'd continued into the dorm and gone about her usual business, pretending nothing unusual had happened. Or she'd engaged Holly directly in some way, acknowledging what she'd witnessed. It couldn't be that unusual to discover your roommate masturbating privately in the small confines of the same room. These were young women in the sexual prime of their lives. Where else could they act on their private passions but in the relative seclusion of their own room?

Holly had reached out to her friend in a vulnerable moment. Had her roommate simply brushed it off as a common practice among people their age and told Holly not to worry about it? Or had they begun a meaningful dialogue about Holly's attraction to Jen and discussed whether the feeling was mutual? Or had Jen torn off her *own* clothes and jumped into bed with Holly to begin a torrid affair?

Either way, I couldn't stop thinking about it all night. I came over and over again imagining Jen sucking on Holly's pointy nipples and probing every recess of her with her body. I wondered if Holly had been serious about running out to her local sex shop and stocking up on the latest generation of toys. The thought of she and Jen twisting their bodies together while connected by a two-sided dildo was too much. I plunged my rabbit vibrator back inside my pussy and held it tightly against my mound as I gushed all over the animated phallus.

The following night, I didn't know what to expect. If Jen had responded positively to her outreach, Holly could quickly lose interest in further contact with me. And if her roommate had shunned her advances, she might be reluctant to go back online for fear of being caught in the act again. She might even have trouble finding alone time this late at night. Her roommate couldn't be spending *all* of her free time with her boyfriend. She'd still need time to study and get caught up on her private affairs.

But there was one thing Holly said that kept me coming back. She'd alluded to the possibility of including her room-mate in our online games if she got that far. *I'll see if that can be arranged,* she said. I wondered if she meant to go so far as to arrange an in-the-flesh get-together. *Maybe we can arrange our own little ménage à trois.* I'd never been with two girls at the same time, and the possibilities with three women made my head spin.

Around the same time the following evening, I logged back onto SapphicChat to see if she was still available. For over an hour, I toggled through the gallery of online visitors, but there was no sign of Holly. As sexy as some of the other candidates seemed, I had no interest in engaging with anyone else right now. There was only one person I was interested in, and my pretty college girl from UC was nowhere to be found.

I was just about to close my laptop for the night when it suddenly struck me. Maybe Holly had the same idea as me. Maybe she had no interest in wading through another collection of online strangers until she found me again. There was a good chance she was waiting for me to reconnect on our private line, via Skype. I quickly logged out of the public chatroom and launched the private app. When I logged back in, I filtered my list of contacts to display only those who were *Active Now*. Holly's familiar thumbnail appeared with a green dot beside it to indicate that she was online.

Oh my God! I thought. *She's been waiting for me!*

As my pussy fluttered in excitement, I hesitated before sending her a note.

What should I wear for this chat? What if she was with her roommate this time?

I didn't want to be too presumptuous by wearing something too skimpy and come off as some kind of floozy. What if she just wanted to chat to tell me she'd found a new outlet for her lesbian affections?

I went into my wardrobe and wrapped a silk robe over my camisole, then carried my laptop to my bed and made myself comfortable against the headboard. I paused with my hands over my keyboard, wondering how I should proceed after our last embarrassing incident. I decided to send her a text message this time, just to make sure she was free to talk.

Hi Holly, I typed. It's Jade. *Are you alone?*

Within seconds, a video call request came warbling over the line, indicating that she wanted to chat live.

Maybe I didn't scare her off so badly last time after all, I thought, clicking the Accept button.

When the call connected and our video windows went live, this time I saw Holly sitting on the bed next to another young girl wearing a UC T-shirt and skimpy panties.

My heart skipped a beat when I realized what was happening.

Could it really be? I thought. *Had she connected that quickly with her roomie and persuaded her to pull me into their affair?*

"I see you've made a new friend," I spoke into the mic, trying to conceal the excitement in my voice.

"Hi Jade," the other girl said. She appeared to be about Holly's age, and almost as pretty. With long blond hair, penetrating blue eyes, and plump rosebud lips, the pair of them looked like models straight out of an Abercrombie & Fitch commercial. "Holly's told me so much about you."

"Oh?" I said, still dumbfounded at the situation I found myself in.

"This is my roommate Jen that I was telling you about," Holly said. "I told her how you've been helping me connect with my—*feminine instincts.*"

"Um, yes," I stammered, unsure how much Holly had shared with her roommate. "We've been exploring some mutual interests."

"That's not the *only* thing she's been exploring," Jen said, leaning over to give Holly a long passionate kiss on her lips.

"I'm glad to see you two have finally connected," I said. "It sounded as if Holly might never break you away from your boyfriend, Jen."

"He wasn't really my boyfriend. More of a *boy-toy* to mess around with occasionally. I've had my eye on Holly ever since we became roommates. If it wasn't for you, I might never have known she was also interested in girls."

"Not just *any* girl," Holly said, reaching out her hand to intertwine her fingers with Jen's. "Only you."

"And *Jade* apparently," Jen said, nodding toward the screen.

"We found each other by accident," I interjected, not wanting to create a barrier between the two lovers. "Holly was just trying to find an outlet for her emerging feelings, to see if they were real."

"I can see why," Jen said, leaning toward the screen. "You're just as pretty and sexy as Holly said. I think she needed a more experienced lover to help her find her path."

"Not to mention how to learn how to make love to another woman," Holly winked at me.

"Yes," Jen said, tilting an eyebrow. "She's been trying out some of her new moves on me. I should thank you for your mentoring. It might have taken us *months* to figure out all the special things we girls can do with one another."

My pussy fluttered at the thought of the two girls making out all night long.

"Oh? You've been practicing?" I teased, fishing for more details.

Jen suddenly lifted herself up and straddled Holly's hips, facing away from the camera.

"To say the least," she said. "Would you like to see? Maybe you can show us a few new moves."

I squirmed on my bed, suddenly aware of the wet spot forming in the seat of my robe.

"I'd love to watch you ravish each other. Do you mind if this old lady has a little fun while you two go at it?"

"We were kind of hoping you would," Jen said. "And you're far from an old lady. Can we see a bit more of your body? Holly said you have an amazing figure."

"Absolutely," I said, scarcely believing my luck having the opportunity to have online sex with two gorgeous young co-eds. I quickly tore off my robe and pulled down my panties, feeling the torrent of fluid between my legs soaking into my bedsheets.

"Can we see your tits, too?" Jen said. "Those are some pretty fine looking hooters."

I hesitated for a moment revealing any more of my body, out of concern this was shaping up to be a one-sided show, rather than the two-way exchange I'd enjoyed with Holly so far. It was obvious that Jen was the more aggressive partner in their relationship, and I didn't want Holly feeling embarrassed or left out.

"Am I the *only* one getting undressed?" I asked.

"No way," Holly said, pulling her T-shirt over her head. Jen quickly followed suit, and the two girls pressed their bare breasts together while they kissed passionately.

As I watched the girls rubbing their bodies together, I pulled my camisole over my head and began pinching my nipples. Jen pressed her body forward, tilting Holly down onto the bed, then they twisted their bodies so they could watch the screen from the side.

"Damn, Jade," Jen said. "Holly wasn't kidding. You have a gorgeous body. I can see how she got off so easily watching you."

"I can't hold a candle to you guys," I said, admiring the

two girls' smooth, flexible bodies. "I wish everything stood as firm and perky on me as it does on you. You've got a very sexy body too, Jen."

"Talk dirty to us," she said. "Tell us what you want us to do. Holly was telling me about some of the things you like."

I guess all pretenses are off at this point, I thought. *It's time to get down and dirty.* I spread my legs and placed my fingers over my slick opening.

"I want to watch you suck on Holly's pretty nipples. Make them hard and long again, like I saw them yesterday."

Jen leaned forward and took Holly's left breast into her mouth, then turned her head to glance into the camera. I pushed my laptop away from me a few inches so they could see my pussy and hips displayed in front of the screen. As I circled my clit with the tip of my fingers, I squeezed my breast with my other hand and moaned at the sight of Holly's teat in her roommate's mouth.

"Mmm," Jen hummed, as she tickled and teased Holly's tips.

"You are one sexy momma," Jen said, popping her mouth off Holly's nipple with a smack. "No wonder I caught her coming when I walked in the door yesterday. You could put any girl over the edge with a body like that."

"Happy to oblige anytime," I panted, feeling my juices running down my thighs.

"We might have to arrange that," Jen said, smiling at the camera. "But right now, I just want to fuck my girl while you get off watching us. What would you like us to do now?"

I couldn't believe they were letting me direct the action like some kind of erotic movie director. I moved my laptop a little closer toward my body and leaned closer to the screen.

"I want to watch you *taste* her," I said. "I want to watch

Holly twisting all over your face while you make her cum with your tongue."

"My pleasure," Jen said. "She *does* taste so sweet. I can't get enough of her sex in my mouth."

As Jen slithered down Holly's body toward her hips, Holly turned the laptop with her hand to allow me to take in all the action.

"You're so sexy, Jade," she purred as Jen placed her head between her legs. "Thanks for joining us tonight. I wanted to share this with you."

"*I'm* the lucky one," I said. "I'm just glad you finally connected with Jen. It's so great to see you together this way."

"You have no idea," Jen said, placing her hands beside Holly's hips and pulling her toward her. Holly gasped and arched her back when Jen's lips found her pearl.

"Yes, Jen," she panted. "Suck me right there. Lick my clit while Jade watches us.

When I saw the look on Holly's face from Jen's touch, I buried my fingers in my pussy and began rubbing my clit with the palm of my hand. By now I was soaking wet, and a huge stain had begun to spread over my sheets between my legs.

"Yes—finger your pussy," Holly moaned as she watched me jilling myself. Jen turned her face to see what I was doing then began lapping her tongue up and down Holly's slit.

"Suck me Jen," Holly moaned. "Make me cum all over your face."

"Fuck, Holly," I groaned, watching my fantasy come true. "That is so hot! You're going to make me cum soon too."

"Cum with me, Jade," Holly said. "Let me watch you squirt while I cum in Jen's mouth. I'm close—"

"Oh God," I suddenly hissed, clamping down on my fingers. As the insides of my pussy began contracting in a powerful orgasm, I pulled my fingers out of my hole and began spraying all over the computer screen. I was so lost in the throes of pleasure, I didn't care that I might be ruining my computer. Right now, I just wanted to show Holly the effect she was having on me.

"Holy fuck, Jade," Holly groaned. "I'm cumming! Spray your juices all over me!"

Holly lifted her hips off the mattress then slammed her body back down onto the bed as she grabbed the back of Jen's head. She pulled her tightly against her pussy while she jerked and thrashed on the sheets. Jen glanced out the corner of her eye toward their computer as her eyes widened watching me gush all over my camera. My image must have been blurry from the juices running over the lens, but this just seemed to get Holly even more excited.

"God, how I'd love you feel you cumming on me like that," she panted, slowly coming down from her long and intense orgasm. When her thighs finally stopped quaking, Jen lifted her head and smiled toward the camera.

"You are one hot momma, Jade," she said, wiping the back of her hand over her lips to clear some of Holly's juices off her face. "I can see why Holly wanted to see you again. This is even *more* fun with a sexy spectator."

"Sorry," I said, lifting my camisole off the bed to wipe my screen and keyboard. "I made quite a mess."

"Are you kidding me?" Jen said. "That might be the sexiest thing I've ever seen. I never even knew a woman could squirt like that."

"Only when I'm really worked up," I said. "I guess I lubri-cate a bit more than some women. When I come really hard, my muscles just push it out of me. I got pretty turned on watching Holly cum on your face."

"You weren't the only ones getting turned on by that," Jen said. "I'm about to burst at the seams myself."

I smiled at Jen and raised my finger to request a short break.

"Can you give me just one minute to clean up this mess before we continue? I'm afraid all this fluid might get inside my computer and short it or something. The last thing I need right now is to lose the ability to see both of you getting off together. I'll be right back."

4

JOINING FORCES

I got up and scurried to the bathroom and ran some water over a facecloth, then wrung it out and came back to the bed. I wiped the screen, camera, and keyboard with the wet cloth, then dried all the surfaces with another dry cloth. When I peered back at the screen, I saw that Holly and Jen were lying sideways on the bed, kissing one another.

"Can you guys see me clearly?" I said, hesitating to interrupt up their embrace.

They turned toward their screen and nodded.

"Perfect," Jen said. "What would you like to see us do now? Hopefully something with a little *together* action."

"Definitely," I said. "I think it's time you got some direct stimulation too, Jen." It was obvious to me that Jen was the dominant one, and I was eager to watch her fuck Holly. "Can you get on top of Holly and place your hips over hers so you're scissoring your pussies together?"

She raised herself up and straddled Holly's hips diagonally, with one knee on the outside of her hips and the other one resting just inside her thighs.

"You mean like this?" Jen said.

"Yes. Now lift Holly's right leg up so you can get more direct contact between your vulvas."

Holly lifted her leg straight up in the air then Jen placed it over her right shoulder, twisting Holly's hips sideways. Now the two girls were locked in a tight scissor position, with their pussies tightly clamped together.

"Mmm, that feels good, Jen," Holly purred.

"We haven't tried it *this* way yet," Jen nodded. "You're quite a sex coach, Jade. We'll have to do this more often."

"Any place, any time," I smiled. "But I think you two can take it from here. You're in charge now, Jen. You should be able to get plenty of direct stimulation this way."

As Jen began to swing her hips forward and back against Holly's pussy, she let out a low moan.

"Fuck, yes," she purred. "I can feel your clit rubbing against mine, Holly."

"Fuck me, Jen," Holly panted. "Fuck my cunt with your sweet pussy."

"Damn straight I will," Jen said, pulling Holly's raised leg tightly between her tits, increasing the speed of her hip movement between Holly's flared legs.

As the two girls began humping each other, I mimicked Jen's position by lifting myself up and kneeling on my bed. Then I reached over to my side table and pulled out a dome-shaped silicone cushion with a vulva impression carved in the top. I positioned the device between my legs, then I lowered myself onto it and began grinding my pussy into the artificial vulva.

"Damn, girl," Jen panted. "You've got all the toys. What *is* that thing?"

"It's just a little something I use on lonely nights to imagine I'm doing what you're doing right now to Holly.

Sometimes I like to fantasize that I'm tribbing another woman instead of just using my hands or a vibrator."

"That's pretty hot," Jen moaned. "Are you fantasizing about rubbing *us* that way right now?"

"Definitely," I panted, spreading my legs wider and pressing myself harder against the cushion.

"Does that thing *vibrate* by any chance?" Holly said, winking at me.

"It does, as a matter of fact."

"Show me."

I flicked a switch on the side of the cushion, and the vulva began vibrating between my legs.

"Uhnn," I groaned, throwing my head back in pleasure.

"Yes, Jade," Holly panted as she watched me. "Fuck her like you'd fuck me. I want to watch you cum all over my pussy like you did on the screen a few minutes ago."

"I think that can be arranged," I smiled, feeling my wetness spreading over the cushion.

"God, that's hot," Jen panted, watching me fuck my artificial lover on the screen. "My pussy's on fire, Holl. I'm going to cum for you soon."

"I feel you, Jen," Holly moaned. "Caress me with your sweet lips. Spread your love all over me."

Jen wrapped her arms tightly around Holly's upturned leg and suddenly began convulsing against her hips.

"It's happening, Holl! I'm cumming! Your pussy feels so good against mine."

"I'm cumming with you, Jen!" Holly grunted. "Press your pussy against me. Feel me cumming inside you."

As I watched the two girls twisting their bodies in simultaneous orgasm, I lost all control and began spurting all over my domed lover. While the girls thrashed their bodies together, we watched each other as we screamed in one powerful, collective climax. After what seemed like an eternity at the peak of pleasure, we all collapsed onto our respective beds, panting as we peered into our screens.

"You guys seemed to enjoy that," I said. "I told you there's lots of different ways we girls can have fun, Holly."

"You weren't kidding," Holly said, trying to catch her breath.

"The possibilities become endless with such an interesting collection of toys," Jen said. "What *other* interesting devices have you got to share with us?"

I leaned over and reached into my nightstand and pulled another toy out of the drawer, being careful to hide it from their view.

"I've already shown Holly how to use my special rabbit vibrator," I said. "But my real favorite is one *two* women can enjoy at the same time."

I held up the twelve-inch-long two-sided silicone phallus and bent it playfully between my two hands.

"Scissoring is even more fun when you've got something filling you up inside."

"Holy fuck!" Jen exclaimed, with wide eyes. "That think is huge! How do you fit that inside you? I could never—"

"You don't. It's meant to be shared with your lover. Each of you takes a separate end while you fuck each other, kind of like a man. There's nothing quite like it."

"I can imagine," Jen said. "I wish we had one of those things to play with right now."

"Well, *actually*—" Holly said, reaching over her head to remove something from underneath her pillow. She held a big purple dildo up in the air and waved it sexily from side to side. "I took the liberty today when you went out for a while to get one myself. After Jade explained how these things could be used, I thought you might like to give it a try..."

"*Hell* yes!" Jen said, raising herself back onto her knees excitedly. "Show me how to use it, Holly. Maybe Jade can play along with us on her end at the same time."

"It'll be my pleasure," I said, feeling another rivulet of juices running down the inside of my thighs. "I just wish we had a *three-sided* version so we could all do it together for real."

"I didn't see one of those at the sex shop," Holly said.

"Don't worry about me. I'll improvise. I'm just happy to watch you two enjoying yourselves. Now let me see you join together using that big snake."

"Lie down on the bed," Holly instructed to Jen. "This time it's my turn to fuck you."

Jen lay down with her hips about a foot away from Holly's, while Holly inserted one end of the long dildo into her pussy. Then she pushed closer to Jen and placed the other end at her opening. As they pressed their hips together, the giant dildo slowly disappeared into Jen's cavity as she uttered a low guttural moan.

"Yes—just like that," I purred, watching the two girls begin to hump their hips together.

"What about you?" Holly said, tilting her head back toward the camera. "What are you going to do while we're having all the fun?"

"I need something moving inside me too," I said.

I reached back into my nightstand and pulled out my rabbit vibrator and leaned back against my headboard. It made a loud slurping sound as I inserted it inside me.

"Sounds like *somebody's* still wet," Holly smiled.

"It looks that way. I hope you won't be distracted if I make a little noise while you two fuck each other."

"Not at all," Jen said, pressing her pussy closer to Holly's. "We intend to make some rude sounds of our own."

"Mmm," Holly moaned. "I like the feeling of you moving inside me, Jen. Fuck me with your big cock."

"This is way better than a real cock," Jen purred, smiling at Holly. "It's double the pleasure. I can fuck my partner at the same time I'm getting filled up by her. Who needs a man when you've got so many fun ways to play with a girl?"

"Exactly," I said. "I told you there was no going back once you experienced real lesbian loving, Holly."

"I'm *never* going back," Holly moaned as Jen picked up the pace of her hip movements. "Everything I need is right here on this bed with me."

"Normally I'd agree," Jen panted, watching the fluttering rabbit ears of my vibrator rubbing up against my clit. "But I think Jade has a slight advantage with that dual-purpose vibrator. How can we get direct clitoral stimulation like you in this position?"

"No one said you can't *touch* yourselves," I said. "Half the fun of using a double-sided dildo with your partner is watching them stimulate themselves while you fuck each other. Go ahead and rub your clits with your hands."

The two girls slid their right hand over each of their mounds, then reached down their other side and clasped hands.

"That's the idea," I said. "Does that feel better?"

"Better," Jen panted, as the girls pulled themselves closer together with their interlocking hands.

As I watched them twist and roll their bodies together, I leaned forward and kneeled on the bed. I placed my rabbit vibrator underneath me then I lowered my hips, letting the pressure of the mattress insert it inside me.

"You guys look so hot together," I moaned. "Now I'm

thinking about that three-sided dildo again. I'm going to have to see if I can find one of those."

"If you do, you'll have to let us know," Holly groaned, watching me hump my dildo. "I'd love to try a three-way for real someday."

"What about you, Jen?" I said. "Would you be up for that too?"

"Fuck, yes," she purred. "I'd love to squeeze those big melons of yours while we all fuck each other silly."

"I'll look into it," I said. "Right now, I want to imagine I'm there with you girls. Can you see me? I'm imagining myself fucking you both over top."

"Yes," Holly panted. "Fuck us, Jade. Press your wet pussy against our hips and gush all over our stomachs. I want to see you cum again."

"Fuck," I moaned, imagining the movement of the animated vibrator inside me as if it were two girls underneath me creating the action. "I can't hold it much longer. I'm going to cum all over both of you soon!"

The two girls clasped their hands together on both sides and pulled themselves together. As they gnashed their clits together, the dildo disappeared completely inside their pussies.

"Oh God, Holly," Jen grunted. "I'm going to cum too. Are you almost there?"

"Yes, Jen," Holly moaned, twisting her head to watch me jackrabbiting on the vibrator deeply embedded in my pussy. "Cum Jade!"

As the two girls began to pull their torsos off the mattress and look at each other with wild eyes, I felt the first wave of passion roll over me.

"It's happening!" I shouted, holding the base of my vibrator with two hands. "Cum for me, Holly!"

The two girls' mouths gaped opened in a wide yaw, then they screamed out loud as their bodies writhed against one another in mutual ecstasy.

"Fuckk," Jen growled. "I feel you, Holly! I feel you cumming against me. Cum for me baby!"

"Yes Jen!" Holly screamed as her whole body quaked in an intense orgasm, her pointy tits shaking like two trembling pyramids over her quivering tummy while the girls held each other with tensed outstretched arms.

As each of us quivered and moaned over our embedded phalluses, I couldn't stop fantasizing about what it would be like to merge together in a true ménage à trois.

If they don't have a three-sided dildo, I'll have to make one for myself, I thought, peering down at the giant puddle between my legs.

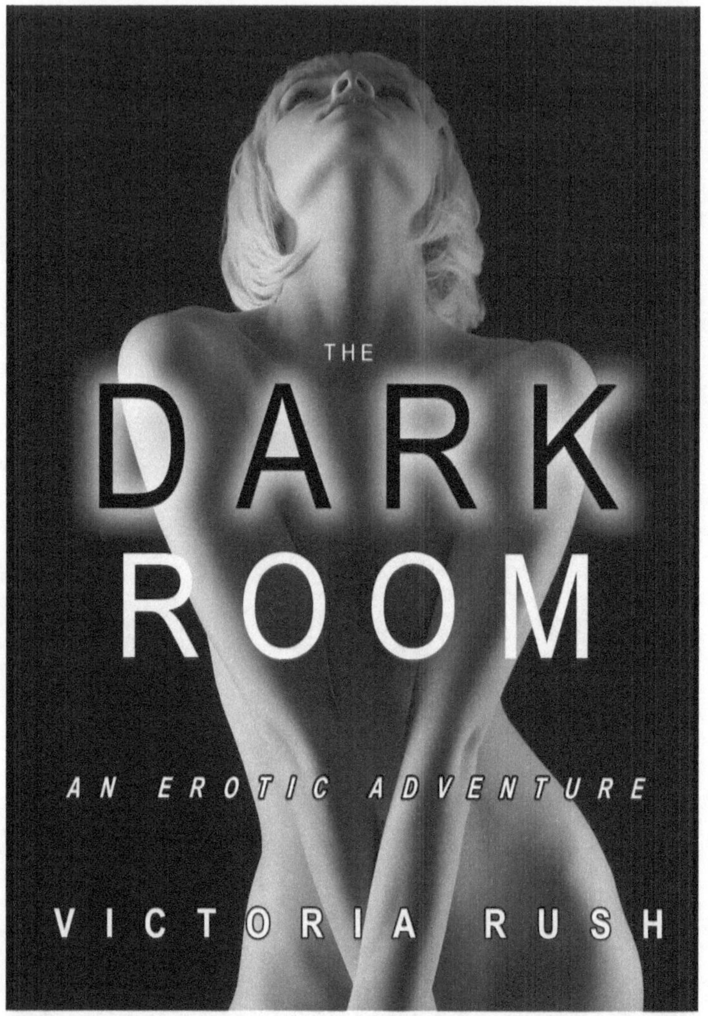

Everything's sexier in the dark...

NAKED YOGA

AN EROTIC ADVENTURE

VICTORIA RUSH

Mula Bandha is for lovers...

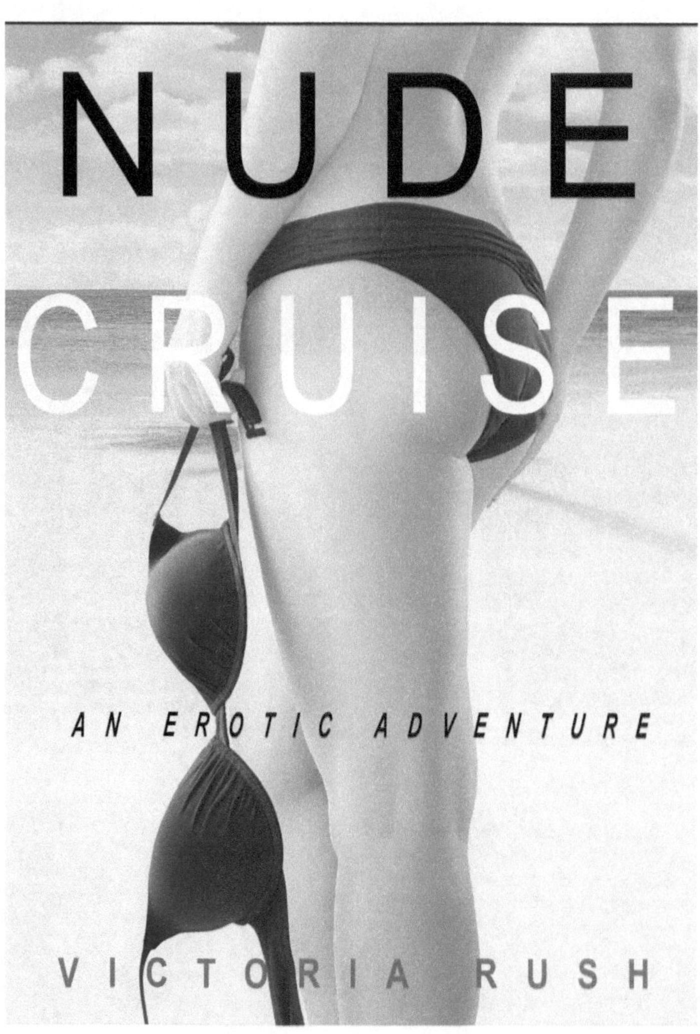

Some people get wet on a cruise for different reasons...

Books 6 - 10 in the bestselling series - now 60% off.

THE DINNER PARTY - PREVIEW
FINGER FOOD

Sometime later, I heard a soft tap on my bedroom door. Not wanting to remove myself just yet from my cocoon of luxury, I called out to answer.

"Yes?"

"It's time for your massage," a woman's voice replied.

"Just one minute please."

I reluctantly stepped out of the bath and quickly toweled myself dry. I wrapped a large bath sheet around me, re-donned my mask, then opened the bedroom door.

A petite young Asian girl greeted me, wearing a kimono similar to mine and a crimson masquerade mask.

Apparently not everybody who works here always walks around stark naked.

The girl was utterly breathtaking. Long jet-black hair cascaded over high cheekbones past pouty lips, her delicate collarbones peeking from the top of her kimono. I could see her breasts and hips outlined by the tightly-wrapped kimono and suddenly wished that she too had come to my boudoir naked.

"My name is Jasmine," she said. "I'm your personal

masseuse and esthetician. Are you ready for your final preparation?

Just the thought of this beauty laying her tender hands on me sent a shiver down my spine.

"Definitely. Please come in. How would you like me to prepare?"

"Come with me, please."

Jasmine led me into the bathroom, where she nonchalantly removed her kimono and hung it behind the bathroom door.

Oh my God.

I didn't think anyone in this place could get more beautiful or sensuous. Jasmine had perfectly shaped B-cup breasts with a thin indentation running down the center of her perfectly toned stomach. Like everyone else in this place, her pubis was utterly bald and flawless. She barely looked eighteen and I was just about to ask her age, but she spoke first.

"If you'd like to remove your towel and lay face down on the table, we can get started. May I call you Jade?"

There was something about her confident manner and tone that belied her youthful appearance. I had no inhibitions whatsoever about displaying myself unclothed to this stranger.

"Yes, thank you, Jasmine." I unhooked my bath sheet and threw it against the side of the tub.

"Would you like me to drape your backside?" Jasmine asked.

"That won't be necessary," I quickly answered.

Jasmine walked over to the vanity counter and picked up two small bottles of oil resting under an orange radiant lamp. She brought them back to the massage table, opened one, and poured the oil into one cupped hand then rubbed her hands together. The scent of lavender wafted toward my nose.

I closed my eyes in anticipation of her touch. I'd had massages before, but nothing as sensuous and stimulating as this. When her hands touched the small of my back, I jerked reflexively from the sexual tension. My heart was beating a hundred miles an hour as I felt the blood coursing through my veins.

Jasmine must have sensed my nervous tension and began pressing her fingers more firmly into my back as she moved them slowly up each side of my spine. The warm oil allowed her hands to glide effortlessly across my skin. She used every surface of her hands to massage my muscles, expertly kneading my skin with her fingers and palm.

I began to relax as my muscles softened and surrendered to her touch. She sensuously massaged every part of my back, shoulders, and neck, applying just the right amount of pressure. Periodically, she would pour more warm oil on my lower back, dipping her hands in it to replenish the silky lubrication against my pliant skin.

Just as the sexual tension began to subside from the utter relaxation of the massage, Jasmine moved her hands down to my buttocks and began to caress them in soft circular motions. My glutes contracted involuntarily and I unconsciously pressed my mound into the firm padding of the table. Suddenly I was quickly reminded that a gorgeous young woman was caressing my naked body. She cupped each buttock between her hands as she massaged my ass tantalizingly, her little finger sliding slowly into the cleft just above my anus.

Periodically, I'd partially open one of my eyes with my head turned in her direction to look at her gorgeous body. My head was at the same level as her midsection, and my mouth watered as I watched her stomach muscles flex and her hips undulate with each movement of her hands. At times her pussy was almost right beside me and I wanted to reach out and run my own fingers up her soft legs.

I was in total heaven and getting wetter by the moment. Just when I thought I couldn't stand it anymore, she suddenly moved her hands down to my feet and began massaging her thumbs into my soles.

I'd always loved having my feet massaged, but nobody did it like Jasmine. She cradled my foot and used every part of her hands to massage and knead every surface from my heel to my toes. I didn't want her to stop, but there were other parts of my body that were screaming for attention.

As if reading my thoughts, she began moving her hands up toward my calf, using her thumbs to spread the muscle apart. She lingered almost as long on my calf as she had on my foot, rolling the ball of my calf between both of her hands, sliding her slick hands up and down erotically. I couldn't help imagining how she might use those same hands to massage a man's erect cock in a similar manner. My mind wandered again to what pleasures lay in wait for me over dinner.

After shifting her hands to my right leg and giving my other foot and calf similar attention, she placed each hand just behind my knees and began to slowly move them up towards my buttocks. Her thumbs pressed against my inner thighs as she glided tantalizingly close to my apex.

I rolled my legs outward in an invitation to move closer. My legs were parted enough that I was sure she could see my vulva from her vantage point behind me. In my highly aroused state, my lips were engorged and spread apart, revealing my moist and quivering opening.

But as much as I desperately wanted her to, Jasmine

never touched me there. She repeatedly slid her hands right up to the edge of my slit, pressing and rotating her thumbs on the fleshy meat of my upper thighs just below my aching pussy. I suppose this was part of her master plan—to tease me mercilessly and inflame my passions so I'd be ready for just about anything at the main event.

It was certainly working. After thirty minutes of Jasmine's ministrations, I was grinding my pussy into the table trying desperately to give my clit some needed direct stimulation.

Just when I thought I couldn't be teased any more tantalizingly, Jasmine opened one of the bottles of warm oil and poured it directly into the crack of my ass. She paused as the fluid flowed down and directly over my parted lips. I almost came from the gentle movement of the warm liquid as it trickled across the folds of my labia, channeled toward the junction where they joined together at my clit. I shuddered in pleasure at the feeling, even if it was only the subtlest of touch.

Jasmine suddenly interrupted my thoughts.

"Would you like to turn over now?"

It was the first time she had spoken directly to me since the massage started, and it surprised me in my catatonic, pre-orgasmic state. I practically flipped over like a fish out of water and spread my legs expectantly. Finally, I'd get some relief. Surely, she couldn't leave me hanging like this.

"It's time for your final grooming," she said. "I'll need you to part your legs a bit further to provide full access."

Grooming? I knew this was part of the process, but somehow it didn't seem fair to transition at this precise moment. At least I'd be able to stay on the comfortable massage table instead of the clinical vinyl chairs used by my regular esthetician.

Jasmine walked over to another cabinet by the makeup table and withdrew a leather bag from one of the drawers, then brought it back to the table. She reached into the bag and pulled out a cordless hair trimmer.

"Do you have a preference regarding your appearance?" she asked. "Do you prefer natural, neatly trimmed, or bare?"

I knew she was referring to my pubic hair, which I generally kept neatly trimmed. I'd always thought going fully bald was unnatural and unseemly, catering to men's prurient fantasies of fucking young schoolgirls. But in this situation, it seemed entirely appropriate, like I was stripping away all my camouflage and armor.

If tonight was all about being watched, I might as well bare myself in every sense of the word and truly let my inhibitions go. I began to fantasize about rubbing my bare pussy against Jasmine's while she poured warm oil between us. The more work she had to do on me, the more chance I'd have to make this last and hopefully get off.

I didn't hesitate. "Bare, thank you."

"As you wish," she said. "I'll remove the long hairs first with the trimmer, then shave you smooth with a razor."

No waxing? This was different. I was relieved to not have to bear the painful and violent trial of having my hairs ripped out en masse. Although shaving down there was always a scary proposition, I felt safe in the capable and practiced hands of this beautiful esthetician.

Jasmine nodded, then flipped a switch on the trimmer. The device buzzed softly as she placed it gently on my mound. I had only a light dusting of fur and it didn't take long for her to remove it with a few short strokes over my pubis. I shuddered as the vibrations penetrated deep into my core. If she had placed the flat head on my clitoris, I would have popped off in a millisecond. Instead, she turned the trimmer face-down and gently swiped the vibrating teeth against the sides of my vulva, sensuously separating my labia with her hands as she moved the device between my legs to trim the hairs on the inside and outside of my labia.

It was an insanely titillating feeling, but just clinical enough to bring me down from my plateau and shift my focus. My mind wandered to the upcoming feast, and I contemplated what surprises lay in wait at the main event. The hostesses had suggested there would be 'contact' of some sort during the meal, and I was intrigued exactly who and how it would be administered. The idea of being fully bald, cleansed, and thoroughly stimulated going into the event was an incredible rush.

Jasmine continued with the trimmer all the way down my perineum to my anus, barely touching me with the trimmer so as not to pinch any delicate tissues. Apparently there were no parts of my erogenous zone that would remain untouched, now—and perhaps later.

She turned off the trimmer and placed it at the foot of the table. Then she took a bottle of gel from the bag and spread the gel on her hands. Using both hands, she spread it gently between my legs, starting on my mound all the way down to my rosebud.

My body almost levitated above the table as Jasmine finally laid her hands directly on my clitoris. The gel had a mild stinging quality that added to the stimulating sensation. If this was meant to excite my follicles in preparation for the shave, it wasn't the only feature of my anatomy that it made erect. I could feel the hood of my clitoris retract as my button filled with blood and began to push outward. Suddenly, I was fully stimulated again and lusting for Jasmine's touch. I fantasized about her bending down and taking my swollen nub between her puffy lips and letting me come in her mouth.

Unfortunately, my satisfaction would have to wait a little longer. Instead, Jasmine reached into her bag and pulled out a straight-edge razor. In anyone else's hands, it might look threatening, especially in my prostrated and vulnerable position. But something about the way she delicately and sensuously opened the jackknifed tool instantly evaporated my fears. I could see how this type of razor would in fact give her better control safely cutting my stubs instead of the usual ladies plastic razor.

With her right hand, Jasmine gently laid the razor on its flat edge at the top of my mound, while she gently pulled my skin upwards with her other hand. Then she slowly turned the sharp edge perpendicular to my skin and began softly scraping the razor downwards. I could hear the bristling sound as the razor edge removed my nubs right down to the follicles. She repeated the pattern in one inch wide swipes on one side then the other of my pubis, being ever-so-careful to stop just where my clitoris lay quivering in a mixture of fear and excitement. There was something about the utter vulnerability of the procedure that made it the most erotic experience I'd ever had.

Jasmine used the same deft touch as she moved down my vulva and perineum, scraping the vestiges of stray hairs away with gentle swipes of the long blade, while sensuously separating my folds and flesh with her other hand. She took extra time and care around my anus and clit, using the gentlest and slowest motion I've ever felt someone apply to my body. The combination of fright and titillation as she probed my most sensitive body parts created a river of sensuous fluids running down my vulva. By this time, no shaving gel was necessary to provide a smooth gliding surface for the knife.

When she was finished, Jasmine retrieved a fresh wash towel from beside the sink and held it under the warm water faucet then twisted the excess water into the basin. She returned to the table and placed it over my splayed legs then gently cleansed the excess moisture and remaining shaving gel with gentle massaging movements of her hands. The warm, moist towel felt exquisite against my newly shaved skin. Jasmine's hands now felt comforting between my legs rather than erotic.

She had taken me on an incredibly sensuous erotic arc, right to the edge of ecstasy and back, to a quiet relaxed place. I exhaled fully and completely for the first time in almost an hour.

Jasmine removed the towel from between my legs and held up a large hand mirror at a forty-five degree angle toward me.

"What do you think?" she asked.

I tilted my head up and studied her masterpiece. Far from the usual red and swollen vulva that I typically experienced after the violent waxing with my regular esthetician, I'd never seen my pussy look so beautiful. Utterly bereft of any hair, my entire perineum from my pubic mound to my anus was totally bald, pink—and gorgeous. I just stared at my beautiful pussy, utterly transfixed by the transformation.

"You have to *feel* it to really appreciate how beautiful you are, Jade," Jasmine purred.

I moved my right hand down, running my fingers along the edges of my pussy. I gasped from a feeling I'd never felt before. It felt smooth as silk: no bumps or blemishes or cuts or bruises. It was almost as if I was feeling somebody else— somebody I'd never felt before. I couldn't stop my left hand joining the other in rubbing and caressing my sensitive organs.

Jasmine lowered the mirror and smiled at me as I felt the moisture begin to accumulate between my legs again.

"It's almost time for your dinner appointment," she said. "Why don't you save the best for last? I think you'll find plenty of ways to satisfy your appetite over the next couple of hours."

She lifted my kimono from the hook at the edge of the bathtub and held it open for me.

"I'll escort you downstairs now if you're ready. All you need to bring is your kimono and slippers—and your mask of course."

I sat up slowly and stepped off the massage table. Turning around, I held my arms out as Jasmine lifted one arm of the silk robe onto me then the other. Then she turned around to face me, wrapped the silk tie around me, and tied a single bow over my belly button. She retrieved my matching silk slippers and knelt down on one knee to gently lift my feet one at a time and place them softly inside. It took every ounce of my power not to grab her head and pull it into my pulsating pussy.

Jasmine stood up gracefully and smiled into my eyes.

"If you'll follow me, I'll escort you now to the fantasy feast."

She didn't bother putting her own robe on. Her tight little ass barely jiggled as she stepped smartly ahead of me. I wasn't sure if I'd have a chance to feel Jasmine's touch again before the evening was over, but for now I was in total bliss ogling her petite, curvaceous figure from behind...

Read More

ABOUT THE AUTHOR

If you would like to receive notification of new books in Jade's Erotic Adventures, follow me at http://bookbub.com/authors/victoria-rush.

If you have a moment, please post a brief review on my Amazon book page at viewbook.at/wc . Even just a couple of sentences will help other readers find and enjoy this book as much as you hopefully did.

Follow, share, like, and comment at:

www.facebook.com/authorvictoriarush
www.pinterest.com/authorvictoriarush
www.twitter.com/authorvictoriarush
authorvictoriarush@outlook.com

Hope to see you again soon!